BEATRIX POTTER'S
COUNTRYSIDE
BOOK

WITH NEW REPRODUCTIONS FROM THE ORIGINAL ILLUSTRATIONS BY

BEATRIX POTTER ™

F. WARNE & C°

Acknowledgements

The illustrations by Beatrix Potter in this book are reproduced by courtesy of the following: the Armitt Trust: pages 9 (top left), 29 (left), 34; the Trustees of the Linder Collection, Book Trust: pages 5, 17 (right); the National Art Library, Victoria and Albert Museum: pages 4, 21, 22, 25, 46, 48; Frederick Warne: pages 1, 3, 6, 7, 8, 9 (top right), 10, 12, 13, 14, 16, 17 (left), 18, 19, 23, 24, 26, 28, 29 (right), 30, 32, 36, 39, 40, 42, 43, 44

All other illustrations and diagrams are by Nicki Holt
Background photograph on cover by Cressida Pemberton-Pigott

FREDERICK WARNE
Published by the Penguin Group
27 Wrights Lane, London W8 5TZ, England
Viking Penguin Inc., 40 West 23rd Street, New York, New York 10010, U.S.A.
Penguin Books Australia Ltd, Ringwood, Victoria, Australia
Penguin Books Canada Ltd, 2801 John Street, Markham, Ontario, Canada L3R 1B4
Penguin Books (N.Z.) Ltd, 182-190 Wairau Road, Auckland 10, New Zealand

Penguin Books Ltd, Registered Offices: Harmondsworth, Middlesex, England

First published 1989
1 3 5 7 9 8 6 4 2

ISBN 0 7232 3484 1

Typeset by William Clowes Limited, Beccles and London
Printed in Hong Kong

Contents

Introduction   4
    Your nature notebook   5

Spring – the season of new life   6
    Will it rain?   8
    Jemima Puddle-duck pond   10
    Watching seeds grow   12
    Nature's mixers   14
    A nature garden   16

Summer – nature in all her glory   18
    Down by the riverside   19
    Creepy-crawly bug hunt   22
    Making leaf and bark prints   24
    How to attract butterflies and moths   26

Autumn – the mellow season of change   28
    Soil detective   30
    Seaweed pictures   32
    Invisible spores   34
    A feast for autumn birds   36

Winter – nature's season of rest   39
    Looking at trees in winter   40
    Nature's calling cards   42
    What the owl ate   44
    A nature collection   46

Introduction

The study of nature is a fascinating and exciting pastime. How many other pursuits can you think of that can be enjoyed all year round, indoors and out, and need not cost anything?

Beatrix Potter, who wrote and illustrated the Peter Rabbit stories, loved the countryside. When she was a child, over a hundred years ago, she and her family had a country holiday most summers – Scotland and the Lake District were their favourite places. In the countryside Beatrix and her brother Bertram could wander freely, and Beatrix could spend hours sketching the wild plants she found.

Even when they were back home in the city Beatrix and Bertram still collected, drew and wrote about plants. They had a pretty good collection of animals too: bats, a frog, mice, lizards, newts, a snake, and, of course, rabbits. The real Benjamin Bunny was a rabbit called Benjamin Bouncer, who lived with Beatrix in her London home.

This book has been written to show you how much fun you, like Beatrix

Beatrix painted this picture of a pet rabbit in 1880 when she was fourteen

Potter, can have studying nature all year round. There are lots of experiments to carry out, and plenty of hints and ideas for nature watching. This is only the start, of course. Once you have done the projects here, you'll find yourself thinking of all sorts of other things to do.

The book is divided into seasons, to give you an idea of the different plants and animals that are about at various times of the year. However, you may find that many of the projects included in one season can be enjoyed just as well during others.

At the start of each project is a list of any special items of equipment that you need. The good naturalist also keeps a few pieces of more general equipment to hand. You'll find it useful to have the following:

Wellington boots	Magnifying glass
Notebook	Jam jars
Pencil	Polythene bags
Field guides	Adhesive tape
Fishing net	Glue

Although nature study is one of the safest pastimes, some of the projects involve going near water. You must take extra care here. Always tell someone where you are going and, if possible, go with a friend. If you cannot swim, it is best not to approach too close to the edge. If you are not sure if the ground beneath you is firm, test it with a stick before stepping forward. In woodlands, do not venture too far without being sure you know the way back and, again, tell someone where you are going. When on the seashore, always go down to the low water mark and work back up towards the upper shore. This way, if the tide comes in, you won't get cut off. Remembering these few rules will mean that you always enjoy your nature trips safely.

One or two projects are best carried out at night. If you are going to do them in the garden be sure to take a torch so that you can see where you are going. If you haven't got a garden or you need to go further afield, ask one of your parents to go with you. It is very easy to become lost at night.

Your nature notebook

Why not keep a record of what you see and do in your own nature notebook? You can make sketches, and write down details of the times and places you saw things. You can describe the appearance and habits of wild creatures, what they eat and where they live. You can draw wild plants and, if you pick some (only if there are lots growing, please!) you can dry and press them and stick them in your book. If you have a camera you could even take photographs and mount them.

Beatrix Potter's notebooks are full of drawings of creatures and plants she saw on her walks

Spring – the season of new life

Spring is an enchanting season. As the sun warms the air and soil, plant and animal life begin to stir again, with a pace that quickens as the days pass. One of the first signs of spring is the appearance of hardy plants such as celandine and primrose. We also see the green shoots of spring flowers such as daffodils. The buds of many trees now begin to burst'forth, and the first green leaves appear. A few trees, such as hazel, alder and hornbeam, produce flowers even before they produce their leaves.

This is the ideal time of year to begin looking out for, and trying to identify, spring flowers. By the time the trees are fully in leaf, most of these early spring ground plants will have finished flowering.

Other events are happening beneath the ground. The seeds shed by plants in the autumn are now starting to *germinate*. Germination is the process by which seeds begin to grow. Before a seed can germinate, it must have water, air and warmth (and later, light). When just the right conditions are present in the soil, tiny roots and shoots sprout from the seed to begin the life of a new plant.

In spring, we begin to see an increase in the activity of the wildlife, too. Animals which had found a warm, safe place to spend winter now emerge to feed and mate. Reptiles come to bask in the warming spring air, and mammals such as hedgehogs and dormice leave their winter nests.

Insects also are more abundant. Many will have overwintered in a sheltered spot, and are now actively flying about looking for food. Others, such as some types of beetles, flies and moths, will have spent the winter safely in a *pupa*. This is a kind of protective wrapping in which the

From *Cecily Parsley's Nursery Rhymes*

From *Peter Rabbit's Almanac for 1929*

larva of the insect covers itself. While it is inside the pupa the body changes its shape, and when it finally emerges it has turned into an adult, complete with wings. Soon the air is filled with bees, ladybirds and the first of the butterflies.

In the pond, the frogs begin their courtship and mating, and soon the familiar frogspawn is to be seen. Frogspawn looks just like a mass of clear jelly with little dots in it. The 'dots' are really tiny fertilized eggs, and the jelly is there to protect them. Soon, each egg grows a small tail. With a few flicks the egg and its tail swim free from the jelly. The egg has developed into a tadpole which eventually grows legs, loses its tail, and turns into a frog.

It is perhaps the birds which are, among the animals, the true heralds of spring. As early as February species such as thrushes are singing to mark their territory and attract a mate, and soon nest-building begins. Once the nest is complete, the female lays her eggs. Some species lay their eggs in several batches; if the weather is warm they will lay one batch in early spring and, once the chicks have left the nest, they will raise a second brood. Other species join the chorus of nesting birds, including migrating species which have left the warm climates of Africa and Asia to spend the summer in the northern hemisphere.

From *The Fairy Caravan*

Will it rain?

Springtime is often a season of rain. The many showers which occur at this time of year help young seedlings to grow by adding vital fresh water to the soil, and bring new supplies of water to lakes and rivers. But although we know the rain is essential, it still isn't much fun getting drenched in a sudden downpour, so it's a good idea to learn to read nature's signs that rain is on the way. Many country folk think some of these methods are more reliable than listening to the weather forecasts!

Some animals do not like to be in the rain any more than we do, and when they sense a change in the weather they will often seek shelter. Horses and cattle usually gather on the *lee-ward* side of trees and hedgerows, in other words the side away from the wind. Cows lie down before rain.

If you know of a rookery near you, try and visit it when rain has been forecast. The rooks, which will normally be feeding in the fields, return to the rookery in large numbers before rain falls.

A few creatures do not mind the

Jeremy Fisher the frog likes going out in the rain

rain, however, especially those which rely on moist conditions to prevent them drying up and dying. Earthworms, for instance, often leave their homes underground before wet weather and may be seen crawling over the surface of the soil. Common black garden beetles can also be seen scuttling about on the surface just before a storm. These beetles are sometimes called rain beetles.

It is not just animals who can warn us of wet weather to come. Ripe pine cones open and close depending on the weather. If the weather is fine, they open to allow the pollen to be blown by the wind to the female cones, but if wet

Beatrix Potter's painting of a pine-cone

From *The Tale of Mr. Jeremy Fisher*

weather is coming they close up to keep the pollen dry.

Finally, don't forget to look up at the sky! The sort of clouds forming are perhaps the best indication of weather to come. Persistent rain clouds are usually low, dark and grey. Showers are more likely from *cumulus* clouds – the tall, thick, fluffy clouds with flat bases.

Low, grey rain clouds

Anvil-type, *cumulus* rain clouds

Jemima Puddle-duck pond

What you need
A fish tank or a large bowl
Silicon rubber compound, if necessary
   for sealing
A fishing net
Some pond mud
Some jam jars without lids
Some pond plants, such as Canadian
   pondweed, water milfoil and water
   crowfoot
Some clean sand
A few large stones
Some wire

From *The Tale of Jemima Puddle-Duck*

Here is Jemima Puddle-duck searching for her clothes in the duck pond. A pond like this is too big for most people's gardens, but you can make a simple 'pond' at home, and have hours of fun watching the small pond animals as they go about their business.

You may have an old fish tank at home already. If you have, stand it outside and fill it with fresh water to make sure it doesn't leak. You can easily seal the leaks using silicon rubber compound. If you haven't got a tank, and don't wish to buy one, a large bowl or basin will do. Don't use a bucket, or anything narrow and deep; you must use a wide, shallow container, as otherwise the pond animals will not get enough air, and you won't see much.

Place the tank in a suitable place, away from direct sunlight or too much heat. Cover the bottom with a couple of centimetres of clean sand, and put in a few large stones. The stones will provide hiding places for small creatures. Fill the tank with clean water and allow it to stand for at least twenty-four hours. (Once it is full of water it is best not to move it again.) Now, if you can, scoop a couple of jam jars of mud from a local pond. You may know someone who has a pond in their garden which they will allow you to dip. If not, your local village pond or any other on common ground may be dipped instead. Tip your mud into the tank. The mud will soon settle down on the bottom, and will help make the tank more 'natural'.

Next, place a few pond plants in the tank. You may be able to dredge some from the pond with your net, or you can buy them from pet shops. Pond plants provide a hiding place for small creatures. They also produce the oxygen which the animals need to breathe, and which stops the pond from going stagnant. Secure the plants to the stones with wire.

Now you are ready to find some animals to put in your tank. Search in a pond with your net and collect a few interesting creatures. Good spots to dip your net are among pond plants and near the bottom. You will soon discover that some tiny creatures are very abundant; probably you will find caddis larvae, snails, worms, shrimps and leeches, perhaps even a few water bugs and sticklebacks – different creatures are to be found at different times of the year. Don't take too many, and remember that some – such as dragonfly larvae, diving beetles and sticklebacks – will consider other pond inhabitants to be a tasty meal.

Carry the animals home carefully in jam jars full of water, and gently release them into your tank. The animals will soon settle down. Tiny creatures will also begin to hatch from the pond mud you placed in the tank, providing a few 'surprise guests'.

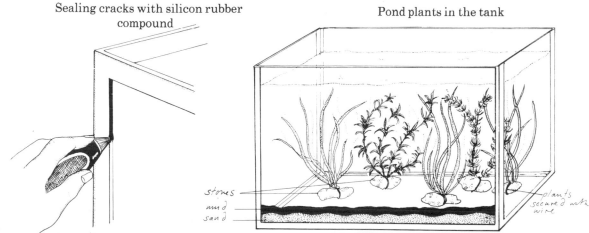

Sealing cracks with silicon rubber compound

Pond plants in the tank

stones
mud
sand

plants secured with wire

Watching seeds grow

What you need
A jam jar
Some blotting paper
Some pea seeds

After a plant has produced seeds, it must disperse them. This is so that new generations of the plant will grow, and so that the species can spread to new places. Plants have invented many cunning ways to ensure dispersal of their seeds, using wind, water or animals, among other things, to help them.

Once the plant has dispersed its

Soak peas in dish

Line jar with blotting paper

seeds, the seeds must have suitable conditions for them to begin to grow into new plants. Seeds need oxygen, warmth and water before they can begin germinating, and eventually they must have light, too. You can easily provide the ideal conditions for germination in your home, and can watch seeds turn into new plants.

First, obtain some fresh peas from the greengrocers and soak several shelled peas for a couple of hours or so in warm (not hot!) water. In the meantime, line the inside of a clean jam jar with blotting paper as shown. (There is no need to cover the bottom.) You'll probably have to cut the blotting paper to fit exactly. After the pea seeds have been soaked, carefully push about four or five between the blotting paper and the inside of the jam jar. Keep the

Timmy Willie eats a strawberry in *The Tale of Johnny Town-Mouse.* Strawberry seeds are on the fruit's surface

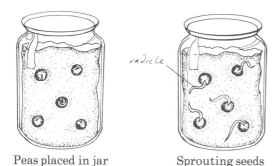

Peas placed in jar   Sprouting seeds

blotting paper moist by pouring a little warm water into the bottom of the jar, so that it touches the blotting paper. Leave the jar in a warm place for a couple of days.

Soon you will begin to see the seeds germinate. The first thing to appear from the seed is the *radicle*. This will become the root. The radicle grows downwards, no matter which way the seed is facing. This is because the radicle is automatically attracted downwards by gravity.

Then the *plumule*, or first shoot, appears. Soon it will pull the first young foliage leaves from the seed. The foliage leaves grow upwards, attracted by the light.

To begin with, the young plant obtains its food from a store within the seed, but as it develops it begins to make its own food using the energy from sunlight. If you place a few germinating pea seeds in a dark place you will discover that they do not grow as well as pea seeds allowed to grow in sunlight.

You can try another experiment, too. Once the seeds have produced their radicles, try turning the seeds so that the radicles no longer point downwards. The radicles will change direction as they once again seek to grow downwards, attracted by gravity.

When the first two leaves of your pea plants have sprouted, you can remove them gently from their jam jar, and plant them in pots or out in the garden. You can then watch them as they grow big enough to produce peas themselves.

Mr. McGregor plants out his newly sprouted vegetables in *The Tale of Peter Rabbit*

Nature's mixers

What you need
A jam jar
Some sand
Some soil
Brown paper
Some adhesive tape or rubber bands
A few small leaves
A few earthworms

From *The Tale of Mr. Jeremy Fisher*

Dig up a spadeful of moist soil and you will probably find earthworms. These harmless creatures carry out a very useful job in the garden for, as they burrow through the soil, they mix together the minerals that plants require. They also help to break up and aerate the soil, allowing plant roots and other organisms to breathe. We can see how quickly earthworms mix soil together, in the following way.

Take a clean jam jar and fill it with alternate layers of moist soil and sand. Each layer should be nice and level before you add the next. Use the bottom of a washing-up liquid bottle or similar flat surface to help press each layer down. Put a few small leaves on to the surface of the top layer.

Now cover the outside of the jar with the brown paper, and secure it with adhesive tape or rubber bands. The brown paper will help the earthworms feel more at home, and will reduce chances of the soil becoming too dry. You will also get more of a surprise when you remove the paper! Find a few earthworms and place them on the top layer in the jam jar. Keep the jam jar in a cool, dark place, ensuring that the layers are kept moist by sprinkling a few drops of water on from time to time. (Don't make the soil too wet, however.)

After four or five days carefully

Place leaves on top

Cover outside of jar
with brown paper

The worms mix up
the layers

Fill jam jar with layers
of soil and sand

remove the brown paper. You will notice that the earthworms have started to mix the layers together as they burrow through them. They will also have pulled the leaves beneath the surface. In the garden, earthworms pull the leaves down into the soil, and use them for food.

If you have any difficulty in finding earthworms, try pouring some bucketfuls of water on to the soil before you start digging. You could try looking for them in compost heaps and in leaf mould, or under old pieces of wood, plastic bags, etc., left in the garden. Another trick you might try is placing a spade in the soil at an angle of about 45 degrees, and then tapping the handle vigorously for several seconds. Do this several times. You should find some earthworms have gathered near the spade.

After you have finished your experiment, return the earthworms to wherever you got them, so that they can go on with their good work in the soil.

A nature garden

What you need
Some large stones or bricks
A small piece of corrugated iron
Wild-flower seeds (from a garden
   centre)
An old basin or large dish or a piece of
   strong, dark polythene

The Flopsy Bunny family hiding in
Mr. McGregor's garden

Many of the places where wild creatures usually live, such as meadows
and woodlands, are being developed
for farming and housing needs. Therefore it is very important that we help
to provide other places for them to
live.

If you can turn just a small part of
your garden into a place that encour-
ages wildlife, then you are doing a
valuable service. To make a nature
garden, all that is necessary is to follow
a few simple instructions. You do not
have to turn your garden into a jungle!
A quiet corner of the garden, away
from swings and play areas, and where
grown-ups will not spray insecticides
and use fertilizers, is ideal. If there are
trees, so much the better; trees will
encourage birds, squirrels and many
kinds of insects. If there is grass in
your wild patch, ask your parents not
to cut it too often and, when they do,
not to cut it too short. This will allow
clovers, thistles and other wild flowers
to grow.

It is a good idea to try and encourage
new wild plants, for many of these
attract interesting insects. Some, like
nettles, may just appear in time. Seeds
of others, bought from a garden centre,
can be scattered in the soil in spring
and will provide food for butterflies,
bees, beetles and other creatures when
they flower. To ensure that your seeds
grow, follow carefully the instructions
on the packet, removing a little of the
grass already in your patch if necessary. You can also turn to page 26 to
find a list of special plants which will

16

attract butterflies and moths to your garden.

If you place a pile of large stones or bricks in your wild patch you may attract lizards which come to bask in the sun. Slow worms may hide safely between the stones. The bricks or stones will also provide a place for mosses to grow. A small piece of corrugated iron will soon attract little mammals, which will find this an ideal place to live.

From *The Tale of The Flopsy Bunnies*

Nothing attracts wildlife better than water! So provide a little pond by sinking an old basin or large dish into the ground. Or you can dig a hole about 12 cm deep and at least 30 cm wide, and line it with a piece of polythene or a dustbin liner. Lay it in the hole double thickness, and weigh the edges down securely with stones. Fill the hole with water and put in a few pond plants. (You will find more ideas for your pond on pages 10–11.) Soon all kinds of creatures will be visiting your pond to drink, lay eggs or bathe. If the pond starts to dry up, gently add some fresh water.

Make a list in your nature notebook of all the different plants that grow in your nature garden, and write down the names of all the animals which you find there.

Daisies grow wild in most gardens. Beatrix Potter painted this study of an individual daisy plant

Summer – nature in all her glory

For the nature watcher, there is so much to see and do in summer it is difficult to know where to begin. The countryside is alive with sights and sounds. In the fields and meadows flowers are in their full glory. In the woodlands the trees are now in full leaf, casting a shady light on to the floor below. Many woodland flowers have now withered and died, but in clearings bracken, foxgloves and other plants provide cover for small creatures and food for the butterflies and other insects. Indeed, by day the air is full of the buzz of insects as they go from flower to flower or swirl among the treetops. As dusk descends, look for the whirring beetles and the flittering flight of the bats. At night moths leave their daytime resting places to drink the nectar from flowers.

Many animals born in spring will now start to leave the safety of their parents' homes to start a life on their own. Young birds will be learning the skills of flying and finding food for themselves. Creatures such as young foxes will be setting out to discover the countryside beyond their lair. Many

From *The Tale of Peter Rabbit*

animals will be raising a second brood of young, and for them the busy days of finding food for their growing offspring must start all over again.

Ponds and rivers are especially interesting places in summer. Insect activity is at its highest now. Mayflies, dragonflies and damselflies are among the aquatic insects which patrol the air, and a variety of other species skate and row themselves across the surface in a never-ending frenzy of activity.

The young frogs and toads, which have spent the spring and early summer as tadpoles, are now ready to leave the water to begin life as adults.

Down by the riverside

Rivers are exciting places to watch nature; there is always something to see, at any time of the year. They have a special magic in summer, however, when the reeds, willows and alders are bent by gentle breezes, and the water seems to teem with ducks, dragonflies and other creatures.

You must always remember to be especially careful near water; tell someone where you are going or, if possible, go with a friend. Take extra care when you approach the water's edge, and use a long stick to test the ground beforehand. If you want to see shy creatures like birds and voles, try and keep out of sight behind any trees or tall vegetation that may be present.

If you sit quietly by the water's edge for a few minutes, you are bound to see plenty of activity. Ducks, coots or moorhens may leave the safety of the reed-beds and swim down the river. Or, if you are very fortunate, you may catch sight of a heron patiently hunting in the shallows, or a kingfisher flashing by in a blur of blue and orange. A vole or water rat may leave its bankside hole to swim across the river, leaving a telltale V-shaped wake behind it.

Look carefully among the stems of reeds, rushes and other bankside vegetation and you may see insects such as alderflies, dragonflies and damselflies. Dragonflies and damselflies are hunters; they hawk up and down the river searching for small insects to grab and eat. Look also for interesting riverside plants such as loosestrife, flags and speedwell.

From *The Tale of Mr. Jeremy Fisher*

Footprints in the mud, especially where cattle come to drink, may tell you that stoats, foxes or even otters have been patrolling the riverbank looking for food. Using plaster of Paris you can easily take a plaster cast of any animal footprints that you find. Just follow the step-by-step sequences in the pictures.

What you need
Plaster of Paris
Water
Cardboard
Adhesive tape
Grease or vaseline
Spoon
Mixing bowl or jug
Soft brush

1 Look for footprint in mud

2 Tape strip of cardboard round print. Push card into soil if possible

3 Pour a creamy mix of plaster of Paris into cardboard ring, covering print to a depth of several cm.

4 When hard (next day), remove cardboard and carefully lift cast from ground

5 Turn cast over and clean with soft brush. Gently cover surface with grease or vaseline. Put cast on an old board and tape another strip of cardboard round it. This is now your mould

6 Pour more plaster of Paris on top of mould

7 When hard separate the two. The new cast will be an exact copy of the footprint

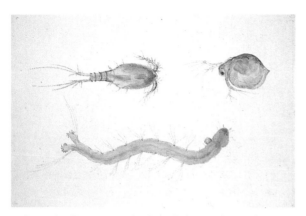

Beatrix Potter studied and drew these three fresh-water creatures by looking at them under a microscope

If the water is clear you may see fish in the river. They like to face upstream waiting for items of food to be washed down by the current. You might get a better view from a bridge. If you have a fishing net you can try dragging the shallows; you could catch a stickleback or minnow. Examine any weeds you bring up; lurking among them may be leeches, dragonfly larvae and other small creatures.

If you have your pond set up (see pages 10–11), some of the creatures you encounter by the river will be quite at home in it, especially tiny fishes, snails and leeches.

Each time you catch a small creature, try to identify it. There are lots of books that can help you do this – you may already have some, but, if not, your local library can probably help. Try and notice the following things about each creature. Does it have legs? If so how many? If it has six legs it is an insect. If it has eight legs it could be a mite, or a spider. If it has a long body with many pairs of legs it could be a millipede or a centipede. Small creatures without proper legs, but whose bodies are made up of segments (looking like lots of rings joined together) are probably the larvae of insects such as beetles or butterflies or moths. Record all the information in your notebook, including drawings of all the unusual creatures you find. Even if you cannot identify them straight away you may find a picture later to help you. Note any unusual things about the creature or its behaviour.

You could also draw up a chart for each month of the year, or for each season, and list all the creatures you found and where you found them. This will help show you how different animals appear at different times of the year.

Creepy-crawly bug hunt

What you need
Umbrella or large piece of cloth
Small spade
A torch, for a night hunt. (Make sure
    you have a grown-up with you if you
    go out at night!)

The tiny creatures that live secret
lives hidden away from view are quite
easy to catch if you know a few tricks!

You can look for insects, spiders,
millipedes and other small animals in
the garden, in the park or in the open
countryside. There are more creatures
around during the warm summer
months, but there are still plenty to
find at other times of the year, too.

First, let's look at what is living on
trees. Many small insects, spiders and
mites live in the crevices of the bark.
You may see some of these just by
looking closely – especially if you have
a magnifying glass – but you will have
more success at night if you use a
torch.

Hang an umbrella on to a leafy
branch, or place a large cloth under
the branch, on the ground. If you shake
or tap the branch vigorously, all sorts
of tiny creatures will fall into the
umbrella or on to the cloth.

We shouldn't forget to search among
the leaves of bushes and flowers, either,
for caterpillars may feed here. Nettles,
ragwort and Michaelmas daisies are
just a few of the many plants worth
investigating. Be sure to look on the
undersides of the leaves, for this is
where many creatures prefer to hide.

Ants, woodlice, worms, centipedes
and millipedes all make their homes
under stones. Carefully lift any large
stones that you can find and see what's
lurking beneath. A gentle dig with

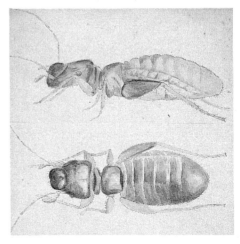

A magnified ant, painted by Beatrix Potter

22

Shaking leaves to dislodge insects and other small creatures

Once you have found a web, tickle the edge with a blade of grass, or blow gently on the web in short bursts. The spider will think these movements are a victim ensnared in the web, and will come scuttling from hiding to investigate.

Drawings and photographs are especially useful if you don't immediately know what kind of bug you have found. You can use your drawing later to check against the pictures in a reference book (try your local library). When you find a matching picture in the reference book, you will be able to identify the creature you drew or photographed.

your spade may reveal more creatures. (Don't forget to replace the stones afterwards, otherwise the creatures may dry up and die.)

Although most of us know what a spider's web is like, it is often not so easy to spot the spider itself. Look for spiders' webs among blackberry bushes, in the corners of sheds, or among piles of stacked-up house bricks.

A spider leaving the mouse hole in *The Tale of Mrs. Tittlemouse*

Making leaf and bark prints

What you need
A few sheets of thick paper
A few sheets of thin paper
A soft lead pencil or dark crayon
A few fresh leaves

From *The Tale of Timmy Tiptoes*

If you have ever examined the bark of a tree you will have noticed that it has a definite pattern. It has furrows, cracks and little scars. The pattern on one species of tree is quite unlike that on another species of tree. In winter, when the trees have lost their leaves, the pattern of the bark is a useful way of identifying the tree. In summer, you can see that leaves also have a distinctive shape and pattern, which is different for each species.

To make a bark rubbing, hold a piece of thick paper (white paper is best) against the bark and rub over it with the side of the pencil or the crayon. You will see the pattern of the bark appearing on the paper. If you can identify the tree, write its name under the bark rubbing – see how many different rubbings you can collect.

To make a leaf rubbing in spring or summer, place a leaf on a table or flat surface with the ridged (veined) side of the leaf uppermost. (The veins are the tubes through which water passes within the leaf.) Place a sheet of thin paper over the leaf and rub over it with the pencil or crayon until the complete pattern of the leaf appears on the paper.

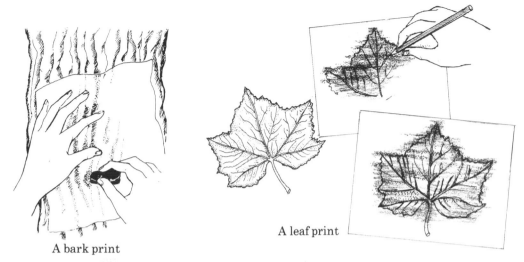

A bark print

A leaf print

Again, write down the name of the tree from which the leaf came. Make as many different leaf rubbings as you can.

If you stick them all on to a large sheet of paper or card you will have an attractive and useful record of the trees in your area.

Beatrix Potter's study of an oak branch, showing the distinctive wavy shape of the leaves

How to attract butterflies and moths

Butterflies

Butterflies are attracted by sweet substances, and on warm, sunny days in spring and summer you often see them as they flit gracefully from flower to flower sipping nectar. At night – even on quite cold nights – their place is taken by moths. You have probably seen moths bumping into windows, attracted by the light inside your house.

The best way to attract butterflies to your garden is to grow some of the plants on which butterflies feed, and

Miss Butterfly tasting sugar lumps in *The Tale of Mrs. Tittlemouse*

some of the plants on which they feed when they are caterpillars. You could just let part of the garden 'grow wild' to encourage these plants to grow, or you can buy seeds and raise them in pots, ready to be planted in the ground when they are big enough. Ask your parents if there is a corner of the garden they would be prepared to let you keep specially for attracting butterflies, and see if you can get seeds from a garden centre or hardware shop.

Caterpillars usually feed on different plants from butterflies. If you grow some 'caterpillar plants' you will still encourage butterflies, because they will come looking for these plants to lay their eggs on. Here are some of the plants that caterpillars like:

Buckthorn (brimstone caterpillars)
Cabbage (large and small white caterpillars)
Gooseberry (comma caterpillars)
Grasses (small heath, gatekeeper, ringlet and skipper caterpillars)
Nettle (peacock, small tortoiseshell and red admiral caterpillars)

And here are some plants that butterflies like:

Aubretia	Lemon verbena
Buddleia	Michaelmas daisy
Fleabane	Privet
Globe-thistle	Radish
Lavender	Red valerian

If you haven't a garden, don't worry. Many of these plants can be found growing in woodland clearings, hedgerows and waysides; just keep an eye out for them. You could grow some of the flowers in a window box too.

Moths

Moths like sweet, sugary substances, and if you coat a tree trunk or fence with sugary water or 'moth treacle' on

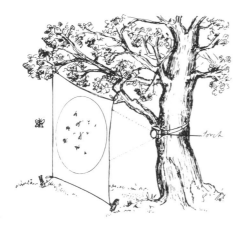

White sheet suspended from tree

warm, still nights you will see many species. To make moth treacle, simply mix all the ingredients given in the list below together in a bowl. Apply this treacle to the wood with an old knife or spatula.

Moth treacle
2 tablespoons treacle
1 tablespoon beer
2 tablespoons sugar

Light experiment
Large white sheet
Some string
Some sticks
Some drawing pins
Battery-operated torch

Light will always attract moths. You could tie a battery-operated torch to a tree and shine it on a white sheet, suspended from the branches of the tree as in the illustration.

Moths also feed on nectar-rich plants, just like butterflies do. Here are some to grow or look out for:

Cow parsley	Scabious
Honeysuckle	Tobacco plant
Lemon verbena	· Valerian
Ragwort	

Autumn – the mellow season of change

Autumn is the season of harvest, when many crops are gathered for the last time, ready to be stored and used in the winter. There are ripening berries, nuts and seeds everywhere, for many plants shed their seeds ready for germination the following spring, and

Harvest scene from *Peter Rabbit's Almanac for 1929*

trees such as oak, hazel and beech bear ripe fruits.

The leaves of deciduous trees are preparing to fall, leaving the branches bare. But first, nature provides us with a special colour show, as the leaves change from green to red, yellow, gold and brown before floating to the ground. Once on the ground they still provide a valuable service: the carpet of leaves on the woodland floor, or at the base of a hedgerow, helps to provide insulation and hiding places for the tiny creatures such as insects, as well as bigger ones like dormice, which need this warming layer to help them survive the winter. The leaves may also help to protect the young, delicate shoots of early flowering plants.

Autumn is also the season for fungi. Mysteriously, often overnight, strange mushrooms, toadstools and other fungi spring from the ground, only to wither and disappear once their spores are shed. Woodlands especially are good places to find autumn fungi.

If the autumn is mild, many plants will continue to flower, and will still

This fungus is *Gomphidius glutinosus*, found by Beatrix Potter in a wood in Scotland

hedgehogs, dormice, frogs, snakes and many insects, must find a warm and secure place to hibernate for the winter. Others, such as squirrels and jays, prepare for winter by gathering acorns, nuts and berries to be eaten later when other sources of food are scarce.

attract interesting creatures such as beetles, moths and hoverflies. Insects such as crickets will often abound, too. Sunny autumn mornings are ideal times to see spiders' webs. Bramble bushes, meadows and grasslands are often festooned with webs at this time, glistening in the sun's early morning rays.

Autumn also sees the appearance of many species of migrant birds, especially waders and geese, which come to our warmer shores to escape the harsher winter elsewhere.

Many animals are busy preparing their winter quarters, and getting together their food stores. Some, like

Fruit-picking in October. From *Peter Rabbit's Almanac for 1929*

Soil detective

Diggory Delvet the mole from *Appley Dapply's Nursery Rhymes*

At night, when the air is cool and moist, many small creatures leave the safety of their daytime hiding places to hunt for food. They prefer to feed at night for several reasons. First, there is less chance of being eaten by birds, although they still have other enemies that they must avoid, such as hedgehogs. Secondly, many of these tiny creatures have bodies which dry out very quickly. At night they are at less risk of this, since the air is cool and moist, and there is no sun.

You can easily lay a trap for these night creatures, and can then examine your catch in the morning.

First experiment

What you need

A small tin with the lid removed, or a jam jar
A small piece of meat or fruit
3 small sticks
A flat stone or tin lid

Make a small hole in the soil and push the tin or jam jar in until its neck is just below the level of the soil. Put the meat or fruit into the trap to act as bait. (If you have not got anything to use as bait do not worry; the trap often works just as well without, since many creatures just stumble into the trap and then cannot get out again.) Make a canopy over the trap, using the sticks to support the flat stone or tin lid. This will prevent the creatures drowning if it rains.

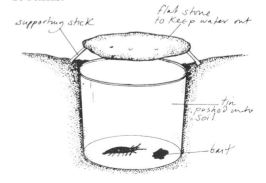

In the morning, examine your trap to see what you have caught. You will probably find some beetles, or perhaps a millipede or centipede. Let the animals go as soon as you have looked at them and taken notes or made drawings for your notebook. You might like to try setting the trap up somewhere else for the following night, to see if different creatures are about.

Second experiment

What you need
A small tin with the top and bottom removed
A dish
Some muslin cloth
Some stiff card
Adhesive tape
An angled reading lamp

Here is another simple project you can do to see what is living in the soil. First of all, stretch a piece of muslin or other loosely woven cloth over one end of the tin and tape it into position. You need to make sure that the muslin is nice and tight. Now tape the stiff card around the end of the tin as shown. Place the tin on a dish with the cardboard ring at the bottom. Next,

put a few handfuls of moist soil into the tin. (If the weather is very dry, you may need to dig down a little to obtain moist soil. Or, you could try looking under old bricks, or under compost heaps.) Position the lamp above the soil. Soon, the heat from the lamp will cause any small animals in the soil to crawl downwards to escape, and they will fall through the holes in the muslin and into the dish. Once you have identified them, or made a sketch of any that you cannot name, it is kinder to release these small creatures where you found them.

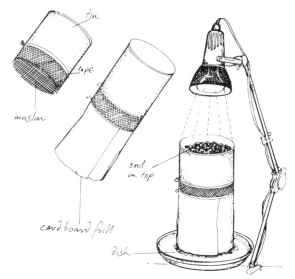

Seaweed pictures

What you need
A large flat dish
A paintbrush
A few sheets of strong paper
Some blotting paper
An old stocking (or cut-down tights)
Some cardboard
Some seaweeds
A bucket

When you visit the seaside, especially if the seashore is rocky, you will probably notice many different kinds of seaweeds there. Some have been washed up by the tide, but many others will be growing on the rocks or in the rock pools. Seaweeds belong to a group of non-flowering plants called *algae*. Seaweeds are the biggest algae. A few types grow to several metres in length, and one or two species grow even longer than that.

It is interesting to study the way in which seaweeds arrange themselves on a rocky shore. At the low water mark, farthest down the beach, grow the seaweeds which cannot stand being out of water for very long. This is the region of the beach where most of the red seaweeds are found. You will also notice the red seaweeds in rock pools.

Moving further up the beach you will find several different species of brown seaweeds. Some are long and thin, some have fronds with jagged edges, and others have fronds with air bladders. The brown seaweeds are

From *The Tale of Little Pig Robinson*

more able to cope with exposure than the red seaweeds, and therefore grow further from the low water mark. At the top of the beach the seaweeds which can live for longest out of water are to be found. These include some of the green seaweeds. The way in which seaweeds arrange themselves like this is called *zonation*, because all the seaweeds are found in zones. Some of the animals on the sea-shore also live in zones. See if you can spot any next time you go to the seaside.

You can make a map of a rocky beach, marking on it the zones in which the different coloured seaweeds are to be found. Use different coloured crayons or felt-tipped pens to indicate the colours of the seaweeds.

You can also make a lasting picture using real seaweeds. Here's how to do it. First, collect some seaweeds. You

don't need to choose very large specimens, just a few different sorts that look attractive. Choose several fresh specimens from various places on the beach, and put them all into a bucket of sea water until you are ready to make the pictures. If you have to take them on a long journey home, put them in a damp polythene bag and keep them cool.

Now, take a seaweed, shake off any excess water, and lay it carefully on to a sheet of paper. Very delicate specimens are best floated in a dish of water first, with the paper slid underneath. As the paper is carefully drawn out the seaweed should stick to it. Use the paintbrush to arrange the parts of the seaweed neatly.

Cover the seaweed with the stocking and then put some blotting paper over the stocking. (The stocking will prevent the blotting paper sticking to the seaweed.) Place some cardboard on top, and weigh everything down with some heavy books to help flatten the seaweed. When the seaweed is dry, you will find that it has stuck to the paper. If you know the name of the seaweed you can write this on the paper before hanging it up as a decoration.

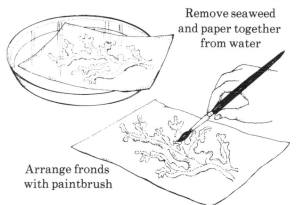

Remove seaweed and paper together from water

Arrange fronds with paintbrush

Invisible spores

Parasol Mushrooms sketched by Beatrix Potter. One is cut in half to show the inside of the mushroom

Although you cannot see them with the naked eye, the air is full of tiny organisms called *spores*. Many of these spores are produced by fungi – the group of plants which includes the mushrooms and toadstools. Thousands and thousands of spores are shed by a fungus, and when one lands in a suitable place it germinates and produces a new fungus. You can easily prove that these spores are present in the air by a simple experiment.

First experiment

What you need
A saucer
A drinking glass
A piece of stale bread

Take a piece of stale bread and moisten it with a few drops of water. Put the bread on to a saucer, cover it with the drinking glass so that it will be protected and undisturbed, and leave it for a day or two. After a couple of days you will see what appears to be a blue or grey fluff growing on the bread. This is a fungus. What has happened is that tiny spores from the air landed on the

bread and in the moist conditions the spores quickly germinated to produce the new fungus. If you remove the glass and examine the fungus with a magnifying glass you will see that it is made of tiny little hair-like strands, called *hyphae.*

Second experiment

What you need
A sheet of white paper
A drinking glass
A mushroom
Clear varnish (spray)

Here is a simple way of showing that spores are produced by fungi. Carefully pull the stalk from a fresh mushroom and place the mushroom cap downwards on to a sheet of clean white paper. Cover the mushroom cap with a drinking glass to prevent disturbance. After several days gently lift the cap from the paper. You will see a pattern on the paper which looks like a cartwheel with many spokes. This pattern is called a spore print, and is produced by the thousands of tiny spores which fall from the fleshy gills on the underside of the mushroom cap.

If you want to preserve your spore print you can spray it with a clear varnish.

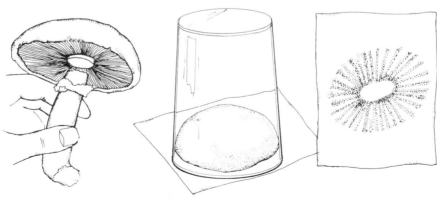

Remove cap   Place cap gills downward and   Spore print on paper
cover with glass

A feast for autumn birds

In the autumn, when many animals have found somewhere warm and safe to spend the winter, there are still plenty of birds to be found. Indeed, many new species arrive on our shores at this time to escape colder weather elsewhere.

Autumn is one of the best times to study birds. Food is more scarce, making the birds bolder and thus easier to see. In addition, many trees have now lost their leaves, so the birds can no longer hide in thick foliage.

Although you will probably see plenty of birds simply by keeping a careful lookout when you are on coun-

From *The Tale of Peter Rabbit*

try walks, or even just by watching from a window, there is a much better way of ensuring plenty of species come to visit. You can build a bird table.

Bird table

What you need
Wooden post 1.5 m long
Piece of wood   30 cm × 30 cm × 1 cm thick
4 pieces of wood 29 cm long × 5 mm wide
A hammer
Some nails

You will probably need a grown-up to help you, especially if you have to cut the wood to the correct size first. (Timber merchants will often cut wood to size for you if you give them the measurements.) Begin by nailing one of the thin strips of wood to one top edge of the large piece of wood (see diagram 1). Don't use nails any longer than 15 mm if possible. If you must use longer ones, be sure to hammer the ends over if they protrude through the bottom piece of wood, otherwise you could injure yourself on them. Also, do not place the nails too close to the ends of the thin pieces of wood or they will split the wood. Three or four nails will be sufficient for each strip. Nail the other strips on to the other three top edges, leaving a gap at each corner for rain to drain away.

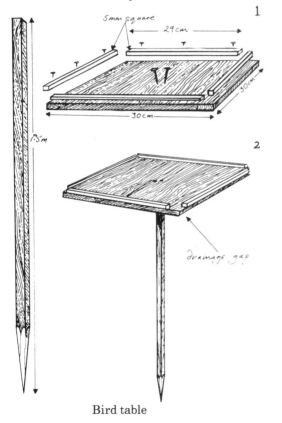

Bird table

Now sharpen one end of the wooden stake to enable it to be pushed into the ground more easily. You should get a grown-up to do this for you, as it will be necessary to use a sharp knife to carve a point, or to use a saw. Next, position the flat end of the stake in the centre of the bottom of the table and nail it into place using two nails about 4 cm long (see diagram 2). Your bird table is now complete.

Position the bird table a little distance from the house. Make sure it is in a place where cats cannot creep up on the birds unseen.

You should only feed the birds in autumn and winter; they can find plenty to eat themselves the rest of the year. In winter, or in dry weather, a small dish of water placed on the bird table will enable them to have a drink – they have difficulty in finding water in winter, as many ponds freeze up when it is really cold. Good foods to place on the table are breadcrumbs, bird seed, cheese and chopped bacon rind. (Some of the food can also be scattered on the ground for the birds to eat.) You can also make bird pudding, which contains many of their favourite foods.

Bird pudding

What you need
Half a coconut with a hole in the top
String
28 g (1 oz) dry cake
1 tablespoon dried fruit
1 tablespoon bird seed
1 tablespoon peanuts
56 g (2 oz) oatmeal
28 g (1 oz) crumbled cheese
Fat

Thread string through hole in coconut

Pour fat over bird pudding mix

Hang upside-down for birds to peck at

First, thread the string through the hole in the coconut, and secure it with a knot inside the shell. Now mix the other dry ingredients together in the half coconut. Pour hot melted fat on to the mixture (get a grown-up to do this for you) and let it set. Hang the coconut upside-down on the bird table, and birds such as tits and finches will cling to it as they peck at the food.

Try to identify the different species which come to your table, and write about them in your nature notebook. You will probably find that certain kinds of birds come to feed at the same time each day. If you do not have a garden, you can buy special bird feeders which can be fixed on to windows.

These can be filled with the same foods as you put on the bird table.

Finally, be sure to continue feeding the birds once you start. They will come to rely on you to help feed them during the cold autumn and winter months.

Winter – nature's season of rest

Winter is nature's quiet season, when many plants and animals wait patiently for the return of warmer weather in spring. However, there is much activity to keep the naturalist busy if he or she knows where to look.

The lack of vegetation means that birds, and mammals such as foxes, deer and rabbits, are much easier to see. If they are hungry they may become extra bold, often entering our gardens to search for food.

Winter illustration from *Peter Rabbit's Almanac for 1929*

Near ponds and rivers birds such as herons and ducks will be seen, and we can still enjoy looking for fishes. Seashores and estuaries are among the most interesting places for the winter naturalist to visit. Many seabirds flock to our shores in winter, and rocky coasts in particular will still be rich in seashore creatures such as crabs, anemones, whelks and winkles.

Snow causes much hardship to animals. Now, especially, is the time to leave food out for winter foragers. For the naturalist, snow provides many clues to what is out and about. Droppings, tracks and trails all help to tell us which animals are on the prowl. Birds often feed in flocks at this time, and even roost together at night in groups to help keep each other warm. The eerie night sounds of the barking fox and the hooting tawny owl tell us that they are marking their territories in readiness for mating and rearing their young as soon as the winter starts to wane. Before long, the first crocuses and snowdrops appear, reminding us that spring is nearly with us again.

Looking at trees in winter

From *Peter Rabbit's Almanac for 1929*

Even in winter, when the trees have lost their leaves, they can still provide us with lots of interesting things to do.

How old is the tree?

This is something you can only tell if the tree has been cut, because the secret is hidden inside the trunk. Trees are often felled during winter, to allow more space for other trees, for fuel or because the tree has become diseased. If you find a tree with a freshly cut stump, look at the stump carefully. You will notice that there is a pattern of rings, one inside another. Each ring shows where a new season's growth has occurred, for each ring is really lots and lots of tiny tubes which carry water up the trunk. You can count the rings, and so work out the age of the tree.

Winter bud cast

What you need
A twig with winter buds
Some clay or plasticine
Some cardboard
Some adhesive tape
Some vaseline
Some plaster of Paris
Paints and a brush

Take a twig with winter buds. (They can be found on many trees at this time of the year.) Cut the stem so that it is about 10 cm long. Now take the clay or plasticine, mould it into a squarish

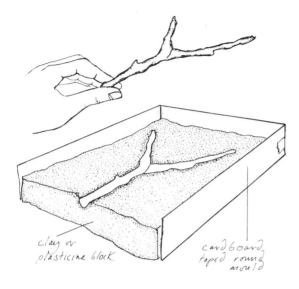

clay or
plasticine block.

cardboard
taped round
mould

a plaster cast of your twig and winter buds. Paint it to match the original colours of your twig and buds.

Measure the height of trees

Here is an easy way to tell the height of trees. First, get a friend to stand by a wall, and mark where the top of his head comes to. Measure the height of this mark from the ground; this is the height of your friend.

Find a tall tree, and get your friend to stand next to it. Your friend and the tree should be the same distance from you. Stand about 10 metres from the tree. Hold a pencil at arm's length so that the top appears level with your friend's head. Move your thumb down the pencil until it is level with his feet. The distance from the top of the pencil to your thumb is equal to your friend's height. All you have to do now is count how many of these pencil lengths are needed to equal the height of the tree. Holding the pencil with your thumb in position you simply close one eye, start at the bottom of the tree and work your way to the top. Add up the number of these 'lengths', multiply them by your friend's height, and you have the height of the tree.

block, and then push the twig into it. Carefully lift the twig from the clay or plasticine mould. Gently smear vaseline around the impression and also over the rest of the mould. Tape some cardboard around the mould, making sure you allow extra height at the top, enough to pour on several centimetres of plaster of Paris. Make a creamy mix of plaster of Paris and pour it on to the top of the mould and into the impression made by the twig. Leave it to set. When hard, carefully remove the cardboard and mould. You will be left with

Nature's calling cards

A squirrel's 'table' in *The Tale of Squirrel Nutkin*

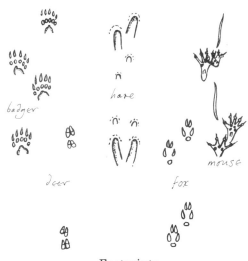

Footprints

Because many animals are very shy and secretive, or only come out at night when no one is about, we sometimes only know about their activities from the clues they leave. Keen-eyed naturalists use these signs to tell them a great deal about nature, and you can, too.

So what should we look out for? The easiest signs to spot are animal footprints. The best places to look are in mud, in snow and on the seashore. Animals like deer leave easily recognizable footprints on the ground in woodland clearings, for instance. Look in snow for the tracks of rabbits and hares, and for the animals which hunt them, such as weasels, stoats and foxes.

Sometimes, by following fresh tracks, you can trace the animal which made them back to its lair. The seashore may also reveal the tracks of foxes, and of course the footprints of seabirds such as gulls and waders.

The signs and left-overs of feeding are another clue to the animals which have been in the area. Stripped pine-cones on a woodland floor are a sure sign that squirrels are about. Nibbled cones and seeds littered over a flat tree stump (a squirrel's 'table') are a sure indication that squirrels are feeding here.

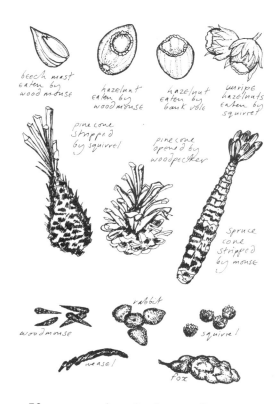

beech mast eaten by wood mouse

hazelnut eaten by woodmouse

hazelnut eaten by bank vole

unripe hazelnuts eaten by squirrel

pine cone stripped by squirrel

pine cone opened by woodpecker

spruce cone stripped by mouse

woodmouse

rabbit

squirrel

weasel

fox

where it has been pecked by a bird such as a nuthatch.

You may come across a pile of feathers on the woodland floor. This is a likely sign that a bird has been caught by a predator such as a fox or a hawk. The predator often pulls the feathers from its victim before eating it.

Many animals leave droppings to mark their territory. You may discover the droppings of a fox left on a tree stump or a clump of grass. Other droppings which are commonly found include those of deer, rabbits and squirrels. You will have to search for these on the woodland floor, although rabbit droppings are also common at the edges of fields. All these signs will help you to make a list of the animals in your area.

If you examine the bases of trees you may discover some nibbled nuts such as hazel nuts and beech nuts. Look very carefully at the nuts and you may be able to see tooth marks. These show that they have been eaten by mice and voles. Sometimes the nut may be jammed into the bark of the tree,

From *The Tale of Squirrel Nutkin*

What the owl ate

Owls are birds which eat many small animals. Sometimes they eat tiny birds, such as sparrows, but most of the owls which hunt at night feed on shrews, mice and voles. Owls cannot digest all of their animal prey, such as feathers, fur and bones, and so they cough up the undigested parts in the form of a sausage-shaped mass called a pellet.

If you find an owl pellet, you can examine its contents and discover what the owl had for its meal. The best places to find pellets are near where the owl roosts. Owls like to roost in old

From *The Tale of Squirrel Nutkin*

What you need
Some tweezers
A couple of cocktail sticks
Some black card
Some glue
A dish containing some warm water

Typical owl pellet

Separating elements with cocktail sticks

farm buildings and churchyards, but you can also find owl pellets in woodlands, especially near large hollow trees.

First, you must soak the pellet in a dish of warm water to loosen the contents. Carefully pull the pellet apart using the cocktail sticks and tweezers. If you find any identifiable objects such as bones and teeth remove these and put them to one side. You may also find the beaks of small birds. When you have removed all the pieces, wash and dry them. They can now be glued on to the card. Can you identify any of the animals which the owl ate?

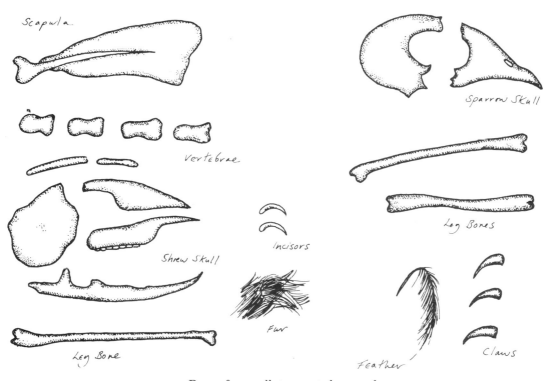

Bones from pellet mounted on card

A nature collection

What you need
A piece of stiff white card about
   90 cm × 90 cm
Some glue
Paper and coloured pencils
Some adhesive tape

Wild flowers painted by Beatrix Potter in 1880
when she was nearly fourteen

Beatrix Potter was a keen collector of plants and small animals. When she was a child she and her brother Bertram had a 'menagerie' in their London home, and made drawings of all they saw.

Beatrix wrote under this sketch, 'Siskin, who
died August 20th 1879'

One of the most exciting ways of recording the nature around us is to make a collection, which can then be displayed. The best way to display your collection is by seasons but, if you prefer, you can divide the display into different habitats such as woods, ponds, seashores and meadows.

Divide the white card into four equal sections as shown, and write the name of a season in each section, at the top. All you have to do now is start your collection. It is quite fun to start a nature collection in the New Year, or early winter when there are still feathers, berries, nuts and leaves to be

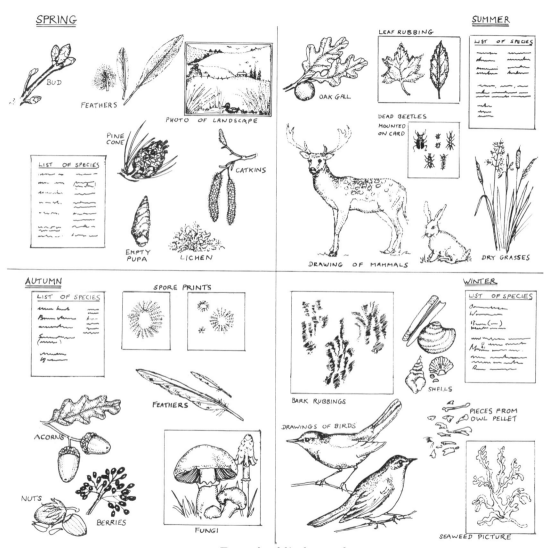

SPRING

BUD

FEATHERS

PHOTO OF LANDSCAPE

PINE CONE

CATKINS

LIST OF SPECIES

EMPTY PUPA

LICHEN

SUMMER

LEAF RUBBING

LIST OF SPECIES

OAK GALL

DEAD BEETLES MOUNTED ON CARD

DRY GRASSES

DRAWING OF MAMMALS

AUTUMN

LIST OF SPECIES

SPORE PRINTS

FEATHERS

ACORNS

NUTS

BERRIES

FUNGI

WINTER

LIST OF SPECIES

BARK RUBBINGS

SHELLS

DRAWINGS OF BIRDS

PIECES FROM OWL PELLET

SEAWEED PICTURE

Example of display card

47

found. Good places to look are under trees and bushes, by hedgerows and by the edges of ponds and rivers. You might need to identify some of the things you find, so a field guide to the countryside is a useful book to have close by.

Many of the items which you collect can be stuck on to the card with glue, but others may be attached with adhesive tape. Don't forget that you can also display photographs that you have taken. Trees, flowers – even views of a field or hedgerow – are good subjects to photograph.

Try to ensure that you display your collection in a neat and tidy manner, and group similar objects – such as feathers – together. When you have identified each item write the name on a piece of paper, cut it out and stick it underneath.

You can also make lists of the animals or plants you have seen, and can add these to your display. Don't forget to add leaf or bark rubbings. (See pages 24–25.) If any season looks a little bare, see if you can manage a

A collection of caterpillars drawn by Beatrix when she was nine. She wrote out information about each caterpillar beside the picture

visit to the seaside; you'll find plenty of shells, seaweed and other articles there to include in your collection. Wherever you are, always keep a close lookout for things to collect. You'll soon have a really wonderful display to show your friends and family.